The

Falkirk Council

In memory of Thelma Lambert
~A.M.

For Mum and Dad
~J.M.

This paperback edition published 1998

First published in 1998 by Magi Publications
22 Manchester Street, London W1M 5PG

Text © 1998 Anne Mangan
Illustrations © 1998 Joanne Moss

Anne Mangan and Joanne Moss have asserted their rights
to be identified as the author and illustrator of this work under
the Copyright, Designs and Patents Act, 1988.

Printed in Belgium by Proost NV, Turnhout

ISBN 1 85430 454 2

The Smallest Bear

by Anne Mangan

illustrated by Joanne Moss

Browny was the smallest of all the bears that lived in the Big Wood. He grew so slowly that it seemed as if he did not grow at all. The other young bears would roll him on the ground and play roly-poly with him and often they would tease him. "You need to eat more honey," they laughed, "so that you will grow bigger."

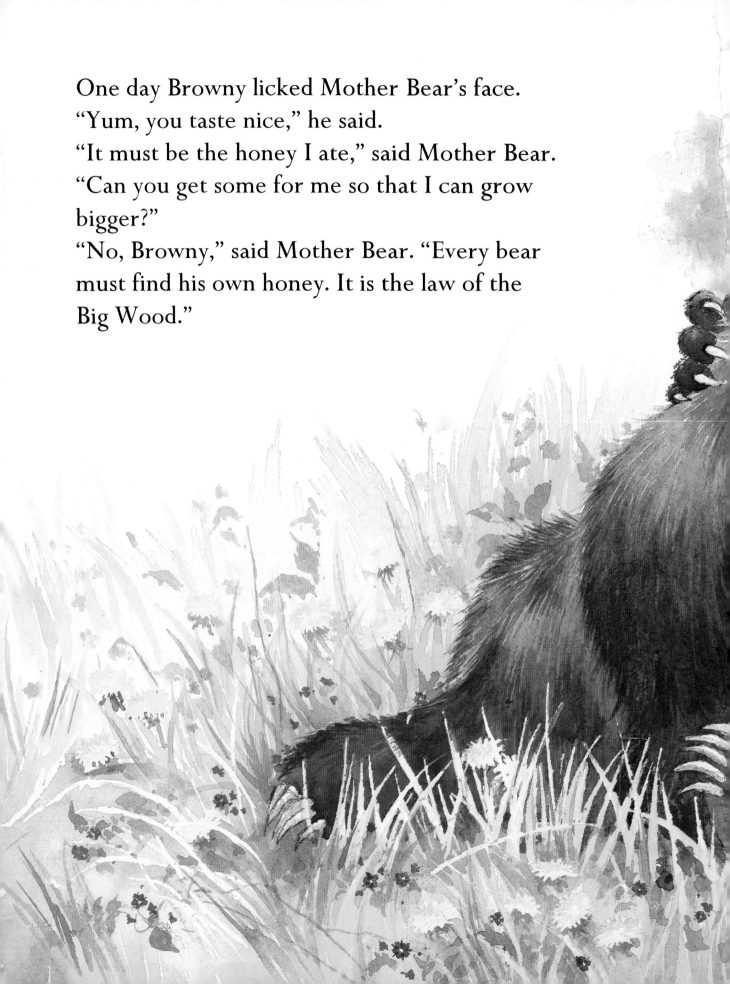

One day Browny licked Mother Bear's face.

"Yum, you taste nice," he said.

"It must be the honey I ate," said Mother Bear.

"Can you get some for me so that I can grow bigger?"

"No, Browny," said Mother Bear. "Every bear must find his own honey. It is the law of the Big Wood."

Browny ambled off into the Wood. There among the trees he saw some young bears gathered around a tree where bees were buzzing.

"Please may I have some of your honey?" he asked them, "so that I can grow bigger?"

"This is *our* honey," said the big bears. "Go and find your own!"

And they growled at him and chased him away.

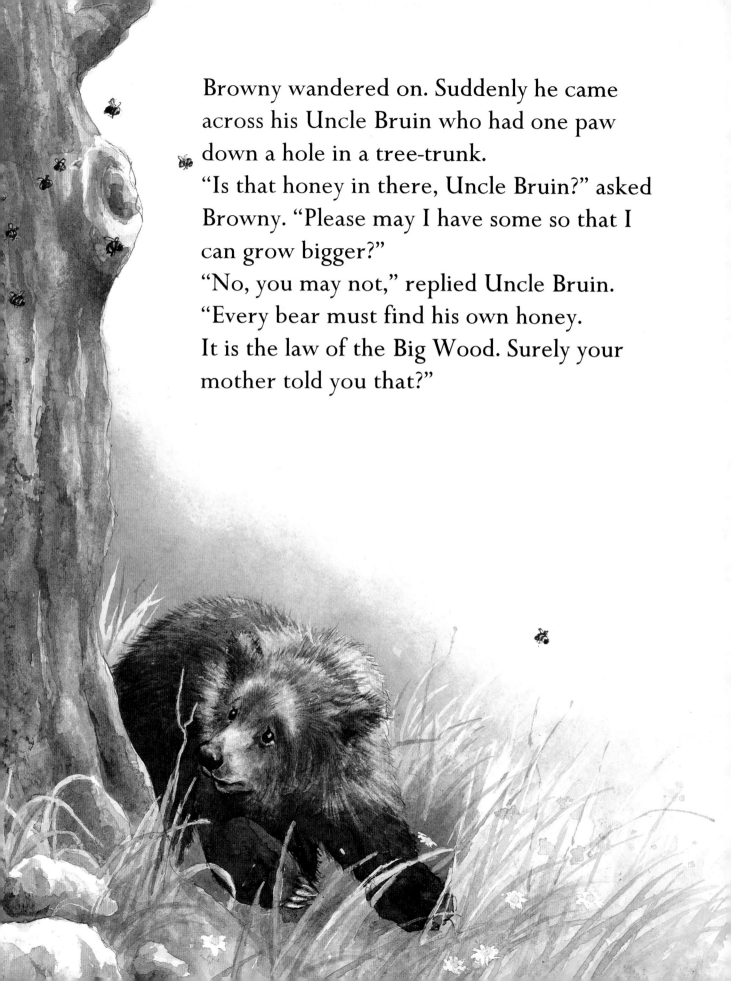

Browny wandered on. Suddenly he came across his Uncle Bruin who had one paw down a hole in a tree-trunk.

"Is that honey in there, Uncle Bruin?" asked Browny. "Please may I have some so that I can grow bigger?"

"No, you may not," replied Uncle Bruin. "Every bear must find his own honey. It is the law of the Big Wood. Surely your mother told you that?"

Browny felt sad. Uncle Bruin was usually so kind.
He cheered up, though, when he saw his own friends.
"We're going to look for honey," they called.
"Ooh," said Browny. "I'd like that. I want to grow
bigger, you see. May I come, too?"
"No," said the bears. "You're much too small to
reach the bees' nests."
Browny didn't know what to do. He couldn't grow
bigger if he didn't eat honey, and he couldn't eat
honey because he wasn't big enough to climb trees!

Just at that moment, along came Mr Moose.
He was another friend and he was BIG.
Surely he must know how to grow without
eating honey?
"How can I be as big as you?" asked Browny.
"Some of us are big and some are little," said
Mr Moose and without saying another
word he strode on, with his antlers
touching the branches of the trees.
"Well, *that's* not much help," said
Browny to himself.

Browny walked on till he reached the lake.
He stood in the water and watched the fish
swimming and splashing. Perhaps *they* would
know how he could grow bigger?
"We only grow as big as we are meant to be,"
said a little fish. "You have to wait to grow."
"But I want to grow *now*!" cried the little bear,
splashing angrily out of the water.

Browny stood under
a tree by the shore
and, taking hold of
one of the lowest
branches, he began
to stretch himself.
"This will make me
grow a bit bigger.
Then I'll be able to get some honey and grow
bigger still," he said to himself.
He stretched and
he stretched,
but he grew
no bigger
at all.

"You do look funny," cried a voice from above his head. "Don't let your friends see you. They will only laugh." It was Squirrel. What friends? Browny sat up and there, coming towards him, were the big young bears who had growled and chased him earlier in the day.

"They'll think I'm after their honey again," cried
Browny. "Oh, where can I hide?"
"There, over there!" said Squirrel, and Browny
saw some large tree roots arching up over the
ground. He was just small enough to squeeze
between them.
"Aren't you glad now you didn't
grow when you stretched?"
Squirrel called
after him.

Browny pushed his way through roots and branches, through briars and tall weeds.
All of a sudden, he came out into a clearing with a lake in the middle.
The sun shone between the trees, and there were butterflies and ladybirds and dragonflies and bees.
And where there are bees, there is *honey!*

The bees kept their honey in a tiny hole
between tree roots, just big enough for
Browny's little paws. He scooped
some out and he ate and . . .

. . . he ate till he could eat no more.
Then he stretched out in a patch of sunlight
and fell fast asleep.

When Browny woke up, he wandered over
to the lake and looked at himself in the water.
He was still as small as ever, but suddenly
it didn't seem to matter any more.
He didn't need to be big to get honey.
He didn't need to be big to be happy.
He was all right, just the way he was!